Coach Cam

By

Jeffery C. Washington

Library of Congress Control Number: 2025902036
ISBN: 979-8-9865579-3-9

Preface

What's in a name? A rose by any other name would smell as sweet. Well that's how I heard it. What I'm trying to say is where I grew up it didn't matter what your parents named you. I found out that people you associated with would give you another name. Yes the dreaded nickname. Like if you were fat, they could call you fatty or chubby. If you were skinny they could call you slim or bones. For instance if you didn't take a shower one day and you had an odor believe me there are many names you could be called. Believe me I know that first hand.

The 1st Quarter

My name is Jerry Scott, I'm married, own my own house, a real prosperous remodeling business, and two nice cars. But this story is not about how great I am. This story is about a person that was a great influence in my life. He wasn't a doctor, lawyer, or even a big business man.

The man I am referring to was one of the crudest individuals I have ever had the displeasure to meet. Some thought he was ignorant, but what I found out was just the opposite. As a matter of fact, I don't think he knew just how brilliant he was. The man I am referring to was Coach Cam.

Gregory T. Campbell, was thin, stood about five foot five inches and had dark skin. Well really, he wasn't just black. He was so black, if you would look up the word black man in the dictionary, you would see his picture. He was the head basketball coach at my neighborhood community center. Everybody called him Coach Cam. To look at him, you wouldn't think he knew anything. He always gave it to you straight. Sometimes a cuss word would come out. Of course that offended a lot of people. They also knew behind his rough attitude he meant well. The One thing he did know was basketball and he knew how to coach. I also found out that he knew a lot about people and what was going on in the world.

I remember the first time I saw him I was ten years old. School had just let out for the summer. Me and my friend Tim wanted to play basketball. The only good place to play was the neighborhood community center. Tim complained to me that the community center cost a dollar to get in, and he didn't have any money. It so happened I got my allowance that day, a whole three dollars. After paying for a soda, I had two dollars and fifty cents left, just enough to get us in the center. I did want Tim to come with me since I knew I could beat him in basketball. I told him I would pay his way and we walked down the street to the community center. The Rock is what everybody called the community center, because it was a big place and it really stood out in the neighborhood.

You could see it from a couple blocks away. It was a nice place. It had a swimming pool, weight rooms, it even had a game room with board games and a pool table.

We walked into the building and went up to the counter and said to the lady at the desk, "Two passes please," she said, "Cams not here yet, so if you go into the gym be good." We told her" ok". I paid our money, and she gave us our passes. We started in the gym because we wanted to play basketball. Tim and I started shooting hoops, and I was in the zone. I hit two shots in a row. So what if it was from right under the basket. I know that sounds very vain, but I was feeling like Michael Jordan shooting the winning shot in the NBA playoffs. That's when I heard a rough and scratchy voice say, "lucky shot." I felt insulted and I yelled, "luck shot? That was skill.

That was the first time I ever saw Coach Cam. Coach Cam laughed, and had the nerve to insult me again, he said "hee hee hee, you don't even know how to spell skill." That made me really angry, so I answered with a smart comment, "I'm playing basketball old man, not basket weaving, like you guys do at home." My comment got other kids coming over to hear what was going on. They all gathered around and started laughing. Coach Cam was clearly annoyed and answered, "You got jokes, you think you can play basketball?" I said boastfully, "Better than you, old man," that comment started all the kids saying "OOO!" I don't know why I said that, because I really couldn't play basketball very well, but I didn't need an old man making fun of me either. So Coach Cam said, "What do you want? Set shots, or foul shots? Name your poison."

I was so basketball illiterate, I didn't even know what he was talking about, and answered, "what?" That's when all the kids started laughing at me. Coach Cam responded by saying, "Ok stupid, we shoot foul shots, best out of ten, for a nickel. You shoot first." I thought to myself, what is he talking about? Tim knew even less than I did about basketball, but he whispered, "he wants to play you for a nickel."

I had fifty cents in my pocket so without hesitation I replied, "You're on old man," wouldn't you know all the kids yelled "OOO!" again. There I was in my first basketball one on one game. I grabbed the ball and started to shoot the ball from where I was, about two feet from the basket. That's when Coach Cam yelled, "Hey stupid, you shoot the ball from behind that line, back there."

I looked back where Coach Cam pointed. I was shocked, it was the foul line, but it looked like it was in the next block, only the big guys shot from there. But his goading me made me mad so I gave him another smart remark, "I know grandpa, I was just looking for your old moves." All the kids yelled "OOO!"

I thought that was a good comeback. I just wish everyone else would stop yelling "OOO!" That was making me nervous, and I was concerned. I didn't know if I had the skills to shoot from back there. I started convincing myself, what have I got to lose? It's only a nickel, okay maybe a little pride also. I took a deep breath and walked slowly to the line. When I got to the foul line the ball felt like it weighed a ton. That's when I began feeling a little embarrassed.

I began to imagine the ball in my hand sailing through the air and into the basket. Saying to myself, Why can't I make this shot? All I have to do is throw the ball with all my might and put the ball into the basket. So I closed my eyes, reared back, and threw the ball. In my mind the ball sailed toward the basket in perfect line and right into the net. I even heard the ball go swish. That was in my mind. What really happened was the ball went over the back board and went into a bucket a janitor left out in the gym. Before I opened my eyes I was so happy. Then I heard everybody laughing. That brought me back to reality. Well I did shoot eight more times, but none of them came as close as my first shot. All of my other shots made the kids laugh harder and louder. I put my head down in defeat.

I just couldn't give up, I had to make at least one basket. I looked up at the basket and positioned myself ready to shoot the last shot, but that was hard because my knees were shaking so bad I could hardly stand. I was thinking, all I had to do was shoot the ball and make this one last shot and then I would feel a little better. It would also show that man that I'm not so stupid. So I reared back and threw the ball again and all of a sudden, I heard a bell ring and then the lights went out.

What happened? Was there a power outage? I just knew I made the shot. That tired old man will keep his mouth shut now. But all of a sudden I felt funny, my back was cold. It felt like I was laying on my back on the floor, and for some reason my eyes were closed. Then I heard kids talking and laughing muffled in the back ground.

I wasn't sure what had happened, but I had to find out. So I opened my eyes and discovered that I was in fact lying on my back on the floor, now looking up at the ceiling. I looked over at Tim looking down at me. He wasn't laughing he has his head down with a disappointed look on this face. After all that has happened, all I could think about at that moment was one of the gym lights were out. The laughter I heard started coming in clearer. Well, what happened? I threw the ball, it hit the rim and bounced back and hit me in the head and knocked me out. Wow, it was kind of strange, that was the first time I was ever knocked out. Well it was over; I lost the bet. But wait, pops didn't shoot yet. Maybe he might miss all ten too. Then it would be a tie, nobody would win.

So of course I had to keep on trash talking. "All right I missed, so what, let's see what you can do old school." I said, of course I had to keep up my rep. Alright, I didn't even have a rep. But Coach Cam didn't know that. You know all the time I was worried about making my shots I really never took a look at Coach Cam. When I did, I saw there might be a little hope for me. Both of Coach Cams hands looked kind of funny. Not funny ha ha, but funny weird. What I saw was he couldn't bend his fingers. Wow what luck I thought to myself. How can he make a shot with hands that look like that? So of course I had to point it out to everybody. I said, "Look at his hands, they look like they were run over by a car." Then I started laughing. But I was the only person laughing.

Well what I didn't know was that Coach Cam was in the army. He had been captured by the enemy and they actually did run over his hands with a car. Everybody else knew that. Everybody else knew that, and boy I wish I had known. There I was laughing by myself, but Coach Cam didn't skip a beat. He replied, "You're funny, let's see if you keep laughing while you are paying me my money."

Wow that was a good come back. Coach Cam picked up the ball and shuffled to the foul line. I was curious, I didn't know how he was going to shoot the ball with his hands like that, but he showed me quite quickly. And like old people do, he had to talk about it the whole time. He put the ball carefully in his right hand and lifted it over his head, and said, "one for the money, two for the show, three to get ready, and your money is about to go."

He pushed the ball up in the air. It flew straight as an arrow right through the basketball hoop hitting nothing but net. All the kids watching yelled "whapp!" Later I learned that's what all the kids said when someone made a basket like that. That's when I got my first real lesson about competition. You have a winner, and you have a loser. That day I was the loser and I graciously conceded. He was truly the best. I walked up to Coach Cam proudly placed my nickel in his hand and said ever so humbly, "I'm sorry Coach Cam." He stared at the coin in his hand, with a puzzled look on his face and said, "What's this?" I replied, "the nickel I owe you." That's when everybody busted out laughing. Coach Cam said chuckling, "tee, hee, hee, we were playing for your same money that your sneakers cost, stupid."

Later I found out that what he said was another good come back. My mother and father didn't let me out much, so I didn't get a chance to talk to a lot of people. I learned a lot that day about competition and some urban slang. For example, when someone says, something was "bad", they really meant, it was good.

When someone says that they are "down" for something that meant they were up to do it. To make a long story short when someone says a nickel they really mean five dollars. That was a real problem for me.

After the kids realized that I didn't have the money we were betting for.

They started talking amongst themselves. They began saying things like, "he doesn't have Cam's money, it's about to get ugly up in here."

To the best of my knowledge, that meant I was going to get my butt kicked. I really started getting worried. For two reasons. First Coach Cam was much older than me, but he also was bigger than me. He has this kind of crazy look on his face, like I just smacked somebody for no reason, so I really thought he could fight. Also my fighting skills were on the same level as my basketball skills which is exactly what got me into this mess.

After hearing all the kids talking, I looked over at Tim and asked him, "You have any money?" He just looked at me with an are you kidding look on his face. Then I remembered I paid his way into the center.

I wasn't sure what to do. I was going to start to act bad and say something like, "yeah I don't have your money, so what are you gonna do about it?" But for some reason, I thought that would get me in much bigger trouble.

That is when I decided to do what my dad always told me, to tell the truth. I figured, what's the worst that could happen? I get beat up a little quicker.

I fell on my knees and poured out my guts, "Coach Cam I'm sorry sir, I didn't mean to call you all those names. I didn't know a nickel meant five dollars, if I did, I wouldn't have bet you sir. I don't even have five dollars. You're right, I'm stupid. I admit it. I'm terrible at basketball. Coach Cam please don't beat me up sir."

Coach Cam looked down at me on my knees, and with a warm and understanding look on his face and said,

"Boy, I don't want to hear your sob story. I want my money!" Well my dad was wrong this time. Even on my best days I didn't have five dollars. My allowance was only two. I was so scared I thought I was going to pee my pants.

Then all of a sudden, everybody busted out laughing, Coach Cam especially. Then he said laughing, "Don't worry about it stupid, tee hee, hee, just sweep the gym floors this week and we'll be even." Coach Cam instructed me to be at the center every day at three o'clock that week to pay off my debt.

2nd Quarter

The next day I was there at three o'clock sharp. Coach Cam told the lady at the front desk that I would be there. As soon as I got there, she told me, "go right in, and get your work done."

At first I thought it was a punishment but after the second day I started to like it. Yeah I had to sweep the gym floor, but I also got into the center for free.

There were a lot of different things to do there. What I didn't know was that they had organized basketball games. Coach Cam ran the whole program.

The practices were during the week and the games were on Friday nights and Saturday mornings, and Coach Cam told me that after I swept the floor in the gym I could watch the practices and games if I wanted to.

So I did and it was great. Sometimes they even let me shoot baskets between games. I didn't know all the rules at first, but I learned quickly. Before I knew it weeks went by. Because I kept sweeping the floor in the gym, I got into the center for free.

At first it felt like I was taking advantage of them. What I thought was free entrance into the center started turning into a job.

That was because Coach Cam started giving me more things to do. Like emptying the trash, sweeping, and mopping the bleachers, getting out the basketballs, as well as sweeping the gym floor.

But I didn't mind one bit because I got to stay and watch the games. I started going every day. As soon as the center open. As me and Coach Cam got closer, he told me to start calling him Cam. So I did. Cam saw me so much, he decided to show me how to play basketball.

I didn't know it was going to be so hard. Even though it was hard, it was also fun. Cam not only let you play, but he also played too. He really gave it to you straight, he said, "if you don't love basketball it becomes a hard sport, like everything you do in life, you only enjoy the things you love. I can't promise you'll make it to the NBA. But I will promise, if you play to your best ability, win, or lose, you will have fun, and that's what it's all about."

First he started giving me exercises like pushups and sit-ups to build up my strength. Showing me how to dribble the ball and of course shooting the ball.

Cam was really surprising, he somehow always managed to have food there for all the kids before practice, good food like hot dogs, hamburgers, chili, and macaroni and cheese, so we could eat and be energized for practice. Cam always told me I could eat as much as I wanted.

When school started, Cam made sure I did my homework. That was before he put me to work. After a while I started getting kind of good at basketball. A lot of the guys would compliment me, but Coach Cam always made fun of me when I missed a shot or made a mistake. Then he would say sarcastically, "you could be good."

I went to the center so much they gave me a nickname, Stupid, well that's the name Cam affectionately gave me. I didn't care because I was having the time of my life.

3rd Quarter

One Saturday I was at the center doing one of my many odd jobs when Cam called me, "Hey Stupid, come here!" I rushed to see what he wanted. When I got there, Cam looked happy. What he did next changed my life. He threw a t-shirt at me and said,

"Hey Stupid, one of my players is out, and you're taking his place." No, do you want to, no will you, no can you. Just, you're taking his place. So my only answer could be, "Ok," and there I was, on an organized basketball team.

Everything happened so fast, so I had no time to be nervous. Then I looked at my t-shirt, it said Cougars in the front and my number on the back was five. Wow, the Cougars that was Cam's personal team, and they were the best in the league. Well there was no way of getting out of this. So I put on the t-shirt and started to get ready to play.

Then I looked up at the scoreboard and it said Cougars home, Baller's visitors. Wow the Ballers the second-best team in the league. When all of a sudden four guys walked up to me and blurted out their names. "Hey Stupid, I'm Cole." "Hey Stupid, I'm Amir." "Hey Stupid, I'm Pete." "Hey Stupid, I'm Ice." I thought to myself, *what was that? Soul? Casmir? Heat? And Vice?* This was going to be tough.

I just met my team, and I can't even remember their names. Cam called us to our bench, and we all got in a huddle around Cam. Cam's scratchy voice yelled, "Remember, we know we can score, we have to stop them! DEFENSE ON THREE! ONE-TWO-THREE!" All the kids on the team yelled "DEFENSE!" I didn't yell but I did move my mouth and then walked out on the gym floor.

At first I thought it was going to be hard, but it wasn't as hard as I thought, because I had watched so many games, it started becoming familiar. I knew we would all get in a circle, and then the man in the striped shirt would blow his whistle and throw the ball in the air. We all would go after it.

I was trying to figure out what to do next when Pete pointed, and said to me,

"Stupid, stand there next to number three." So I moved where I was told to go., Then Ice said to me, "Hey Stupid, you've got number three, don't let him get the ball." Number three was a little shorter than me. He smiled and said, "Good luck." I thought to myself, *this guy wasn't that bad.*"

It's a funny thing, even though I saw about a thousand games, it felt different actually being on the court. It's a completely different perspective.

Then the man in the striped shirt walks out on the floor with the ball. He blew his whistle. That meant the game was about to start. The man in the striped shirt pointed to my right and said, "Cougars basket." Then he pointed to my left and said, "Baller's basket."

I was ready to go, the man in the striped shirt walked to the middle of the floor and threw the ball in the air. The Ballers guy jumped in the air and tapped the ball to number three and off he ran dribbling the ball down the floor, laid the ball against the back board and it went right into the basket.

All the Cougars yelled, "STUPID, you weren't supposed to let number three get the ball!" Cam yelled, "Shake it off, get it back." Number three psyched me out, looking so innocent, he just couldn't wait to embarrass me. I really should have paid more attention, that's when I realized just shooting the ball wasn't all there was to playing basketball. I had to start listening to my teammates, and remember what Cam said, we have to play defense. Especially me since I let them get the first basket.

After that I started getting my head in the game. I was on number three like stink on poop. For the next five minutes number three never touched the ball. When he did finally get the ball I wouldn't let him get off a good shot. So that first layup didn't mean a thing.

Then number three started getting frustrated, he also complained to the man in the striped shirt saying, "He's fouling me!" That made me feel good, because it meant I was doing my job, it also helped us keep ahead in the game.

The game was action packed, kids jumping in the air, rolling around on the floor, putting up some great shots.

Then all of a sudden I heard a loud buzzer. **BRRRRRR!** It was half-time.

I was concentrating so much on playing I didn't even look at the clock, or the scoreboard the whole time. Then I looked up and saw the score, Cougars 23, Ballers 20. This was a close game. We then walked over to our bench and there was Cam waiting on us. Every time I practiced with Cam he was always busting on me, or telling me what I was doing wrong, so I was just waiting on the usual bad criticism. Then what Cam said next was surprising to me. Cam said with a scratchy energetic voice, "Ok guys, good job, keep up the pressure. One more half to go."

Then he looked at me and said, "Stupid, they're not watching you, if you see an opening take a shot."

That's when I realized I hadn't taken a shot during the entire first half of the game. All I did was stop number three from getting the ball and passing the ball to my teammates. It hadn't occurred to me that I hadn't taken a shot, but Cam sure did notice.

The second half started, and it was on again. We were playing hard and so were the Ballers. They even managed to take the lead for a brief period of time. Ice brought us back with a couple of three-point shots. Number three was mad because he wasn't playing well then they took him out and replaced him with number seven, but he got the same exact treatment from me.

The game went on, back and forth, both teams playing hard. I heard a parent on the side line say this was one of the best games he had ever seen.

The game was in the final minutes, I had not taken a shot yet. I just never had the chance. The Ballers were getting desperate, they started shooting three pointers every time they got the ball. But lucky for us they missed more of them. I was so excited I really wasn't getting tired, but Cole and Amir were beat. They started making mistakes, some very costly ones. They let the kids they were guarding make some easy baskets, putting the Ballers ahead by one at the very worst time there were only ten seconds to go in the game. That is when Cam called a time out.

Now I knew Cam was going to start yelling at us, but Cam brought us together and said in a loud scratchy voice,

"Relax fellas we got this, I told you in the beginning of the game we could score, well now's the time, all we need is one shot. Cole set a pick for Ice. Ice drop it so we can go home."

Then he winked and said, "Get out there!" Wow, all this time I thought Cam was such a big mouth, but he's not like that today. For some reason I felt better, but that feeling quickly ended with the next thing Cam said, he called me over and whispered,

"Stupid, that speech was for the other team, they have been watching Ice for the whole game, leaving you all alone, when Ice gets the ball he is going to give it to you. Shoot it, then at least you can say you shot the ball today, I don't care if it goes in or not, ok." And he winked again, all I could say was, "Okay."

Well here we go, all the Ballers were looking at Ice, and Ice was smiling from ear to ear like he was so happy. He could afford to be happy he knew he didn't have to shoot the ball. The man in the striped shirt threw Pete the ball, and it started, Pete threw it in to Amir, he dribbled it down the court, about that time Cole set a great pick for Ice, leaving him open for an instant. That's when Amir passed the ball to Ice. At that time three of the Ballers surrounded Ice making it impossible for him to shoot, and just like Cam said I was there all by myself. Just like Cam said Ice passed me the ball, surprising all the Ballers.

I remember the count down like this. Pete threw it in to Amir, TEN! NINE! EIGHT!

Cole setting the pick, SEVEN! SIX! Amir passing the ball to Ice, FIVE! FOUR! THREE!

Ice faking the shot, then passing it to me, TWO! I caught the ball and took the shot. ONE! The ball went high in the air, and it hit the rim, bouncing it straight up in the air. Everybody in the Gym gasped. Then the buzzer went off. **BRRRRRR!** Suddenly the ball came down right through the net, then the man in the striped shirt yelled, "IT COUNTS!" the whole gym roared.

My teammates started cheering. The Ballers put their heads down and walked to their bench.

Then my teammates ran over to me and knocked me down. They started jumping on me and yelling, "STU-PID! STU-PID! STU-PID!"

I just can't tell you how that felt to me. I guess the only word I can use is happy.

Through all the cheering people, I looked over at Cam. He wasn't yelling or celebrating, he just started cleaning and picking up the trash around the bench and started getting ready for the next game.

4th Quarter

We went on to go undefeated that year, and we even won the championship and it felt great. I kept going to the center for years after that and I played on many of Cam's teams. I remember that every game we played Cam always made you feel special.

Thirty years went by, I was riding in my car, and I saw the old center. I decided to stop in. The lady at the desk had been replaced by a young girl now. I explained to her that I used to play there when I was young. I asked if I could take a look around the place. She said I could. I immediatcly headed towards the gym. The walls were painted, the gym floor had been replaced. It brough back so many memories.

While I was reminiscing I heard an old scratchy voice say,

"Best out of ten for a nickel," I looked across the gym and there was Cam, sitting on a chair. He was still black as ever and just as cruel, he said.

"how's it going Stupid?" I laughed and walked over to greet him with a hug. I said, "Cam! I can't believe it, you're still here." He said,

"Yeah, I'm still here." I'm not sure how it would be possible, but he looked even skinnier than before. I could tell that he wasn't doing too well. Not just by his appearance but he was also coughing and breathing kind of funny.

Then he told me he was still running the basketball league there. He then explained to me he wasn't feeling so good, and would I mind sweeping the gym floor for him.

That's when I knew he wasn't feeling good, because that was the first time Cam ever asked me to do anything. So how could I say no?

It actually felt like old times. Pushing that old dust mop, up and down the court. As I worked, Cam and I talked about basketball. Time just flew, I didn't realize it, but it was time for practice, and in about a hot minute the whole gym was invaded by kids all ages, colors and sizes, all yelling, "Coach Cam, Coach Cam."

That really brought back memories. Back then I thought I was the only kid that was sneaking into the center for free, but the truth was Cam let a lot of kids into the center for free.

He did that to keep them off the street. Also Cam made sure all the kids that came to the center had passing grades. What I didn't know was that if you didn't have good grades he would get you into the tutoring program in the center. He said, "I don't coach no dummies."

He also made sure the kids were fed. He said he didn't want any kids to grow up hungry like he was as a kid. He told me before he went into the army, he loved to play basketball. And that playing basketball at the center was the only thing that kept him out of trouble. I saw a tear come out of his eye when he remembered a lot of his friends were shot in gang related violence, because they chose not to go to the center.

Then Coach Cam surprised me and told me why he wanted me to make that last shot of the game. He said, because he wanted me to get confidence, he knew I didn't have it when we made the bet. After all the practice I had shooting, he knew I could make it. Also because he wanted to win. That explained a lot of things, but I had to ask him why he never cheered after the game?

He said because he never had time for cheering, he had too many games to run. He explained to me, if he cheered for one kid, that meant he wasn't cheering for the other kids. He felt all the kids were the same, it didn't matter if they won, or they lost. He just stood waiting for the next game.

I found out all that after that practice that night when I took Coach Cam out for dinner, and he did what he always did. He gave it to me straight. You know that shot did give me confidence, enough to succeed in life, and to write this story. Two days later Coach Cam died due to complications from Muscular Dystrophy.

The year we won the championship we had a team dinner. I even got a trophy. It had an inscription on the name that said:

"To Stupid, Our MVP, Cam."

"Coach Cam, you will be missed."

The End